For my little Else.
A kiss from your giant. ~ C.N.

Clarion Books
a Houghton Mifflin Company imprint
215 Park Avenue South, New York, NY 10003
Text copyright © 2004 by Carl Norac
Illustrations copyright © 2004 by Ingrid Godon
First published in the United Kingdom in 2004 by Macmillan Children's Books, a division of Macmillan Publishers Ltd., United Kingdom.
First American edition, 2005.

The illustrations were executed in paint and pastels on textured paper.
The text was set in 35-point Pastonshi MT Regular.

For information about permission to reproduce selections from this book, write to Permissions,
Houghton Mifflin Company, 215 Park Avenue South, New York, NY 10003.

www.houghtonmifflinbooks.com

Printed in Belgium.

Library of Congress Cataloging-in-Publication Data
Norac, Carl.
My daddy is a giant / Carl Norac ; illustrated by Ingrid Godon.—1st American ed.
p. cm.
Summary: A little boy's father seems so large to him that he needs a ladder to cuddle
him and birds nest in his father's hair.
ISBN 0-618-44399-1
[1. Fathers and sons—Fiction. 2. Size perception—Fiction.] I. Godon, Ingrid, ill. II. Title.
PZ7.N775115My 2005
[E]—dc22   2004012093

ISBN-13: 978-0-618-44399-4
ISBN-10: 0-618-44399-1
10 9 8 7 6 5 4 3 2 1

My Daddy Is A GIANT

by Carl Norac

Illustrated by Ingrid Godon

CLARION BOOKS · NEW YORK

My daddy is a giant.
When I want to cuddle him,
I have to climb a ladder.

When we play hide-and-seek,
my daddy has to hide
behind a mountain.

And when the clouds are tired, they come and sleep on my daddy's shoulders.

When my daddy sneezes,
it's like a hurricane.
It blows the sea away.

When my daddy laughs,

it's like another hurricane.

All the leaves fly off the trees.

Birds love my daddy.
They make their nests
in his hair.

When we play soccer,
my daddy always wins.

He can kick the ball as high as the moon.

But I always beat him at marbles.

His fingers are
much too big.

I like it when my daddy says,

"You're getting as tall as me!"

When my daddy runs,

the ground shakes

as if it's scared.

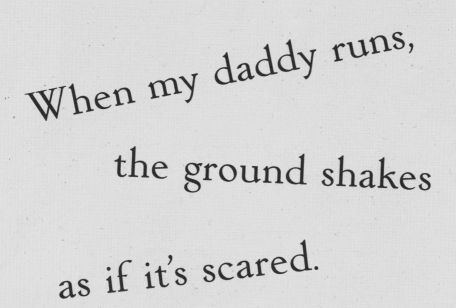

But I'm not scared
of anything when
I'm in my daddy's arms.

My daddy is a giant,
and when I grow up,
I'm going to be a giant too.